THE GERM OF DEATH

BY

ARTHUR B. REEVE

British Library Cataloguing-in-Publication Data
A catalogue record for this book is available from the
British Library

Arthur Benjamin Reeve

Arthur Benjamin Reeve was born on 15th October 1880 in New York, USA.

Reeve received his University education at Princeton and upon graduating enrolled at the New York Law School. However, his career was not destined to be in the field of Law. Between 1910 and 1918 he produced 82 short stories for Cosmopolitan magazine featuring his super-sleuth Professor Craig Kennedy. Kennedy is sometimes referred to as "The American Sherlock Holmes" due to his astounding ability at crime solving and his Watson-like sidekick Walter Jameson, a newspaper reporter. These characters featured in 18 novels, some of which were pseudo-novels stitched together from various short stories.

During this period he also began authoring screenplays, beginning with *The Exploits of Elaine* (1914). By the end of this decade his film career was at its peak with his name appearing on seven films, most of them serials and three of them starring Harry Houdini. Due to the film industry's migration to the west coast of America and Reeve's desire to remain in the east he produced less and less work for film. However, in 1927 he entered into a contract to write film scenarios for notorious millionaire-murderer, Harry K. Thaw, on the subject of fake spiritualists. The deal resulted in a lawsuit when Thaw refused to pay. In late 1928, Reeve declared bankruptcy.

Reeve continued to write detective stories for pulp magazines, but also covered many celebrated crime cases for various newspapers, including the murder of William Desmond Taylor, and the trial of Lindbergh baby kidnapper, Bruno Hauptmann. During the 1930s he became an anti-rackets crusader and produced a work of history on the subject titled *The Golden Age of Crime* (1931).

In 1932 he moved to Trenton to be near his alma mater. He died on 9th August 1936.

THE GERM OF DEATH

By this time I was becoming used to Kennedy's strange visitors and, in fact, had begun to enjoy keenly the uncertainty of not knowing just what to expect from them next. Still, I was hardly prepared one evening to see a tall, nervous foreigner stalk noiselessly and unannounced into our apartment and hand his card to Kennedy without saying a word.

"Dr. Nicholas Kharkoff - hum - er, Jameson, you must have forgotten to latch the door. Well, Dr. Kharkoff, what can I do for you? It is evident something has upset you."

The tall Russian put his forefinger to his lips and, taking one of our good chairs, placed it by the door. Then he stood on it and peered cautiously through the transom into the hallway. "I think I eluded him this time," he exclaimed, as he nervously took a seat. "Professor Kennedy, I am being followed. Every step that I take somebody shadows me, from the moment I leave my office until I return. It is enough to drive me mad. But that is only one reason why I have come here to-night. I believe that I can trust you as a friend of justice - a friend of Russian freedom?"

He had included me in his earnest but somewhat vague query, so that I did not withdraw. Somehow, apparently, he had heard of Kennedy's rather liberal political views.

3

"It is about Vassili Saratovsky, the father of the Russian revolution, as we call him, that I have come to consult you," he continued quickly. "Just two weeks ago he was taken ill. It came on suddenly, a violent fever which continued for a week. Then he seemed to grow better, after the crisis had passed, and even attended a meeting of our central committee the other night. But in the meantime Olga Samarova, the little Russian dancer, whom you have perhaps seen, fell ill in the same way. Samarova is an ardent revolutionist, you know. This morning the servant at my own home on East Broadway was also stricken, and - who knows? - perhaps it will be my turn next. For to-night Saratovsky had an even more violent return of the fever, with intense shivering, excruciating pains in the limbs, and delirious headache. It is not like anything I ever saw before. Can you look into the case before it grows any worse, Professor?"

Again the Russian got on the chair and looked over the transom to be sure that he was not being overheard.

"I shall be only too glad to help you in any way I can," returned Kennedy, his manner expressing the genuine interest that he never feigned over a particularly knotty problem in science and crime. "I had the pleasure of meeting Saratovsky once in London. I shall try to see him the first thing in the morning."

Dr. Kharkoff's face fell. "I had hoped you would see him to-night. If anything should happen -"

"Is it as urgent as that?"

"I believe it is," whispered Kharkoff, leaning forward earnestly. "We can call a taxicab - it will not take long, sir. Consider, there are many lives possibly at stake," he pleaded.

"Very well, I will go," consented Kennedy.

At the street door Kharkoff stopped short and drew Kennedy back. "Look - across the street in the shadow. There is the man. If I start toward him he will disappear; he is very clever. He followed me from Saratovsky's here, and has been waiting for me to come out."

"There are two taxicabs waiting at the stand," suggested Kennedy. "Doctor, you jump in the first, and Jameson and I will take the second. Then he can't follow us."

It was done in a moment, and we were whisked away, to the chagrin of the figure, which glided impotently out of the shadow in vain pursuit, too late even to catch the number of the cab.

"A promising adventure," commented Kennedy, as we bumped along over New York's uneven asphalt. "Have you ever met Saratovsky?"

"No," I replied dubiously. "Will you guarantee that he will not blow us up with a bomb?"

"Grandmother!" replied Craig. "Why, Walter, he is the most gentle, engaging old philosopher - "

"That ever cut a throat or scuttled a ship?" I interrupted.

"On the contrary," insisted Kennedy, somewhat nettled, "he is a patriarch, respected by every faction of the revolutionists, from the fighting organisation to the believers in non-resistance and Tolstoy. I tell you, Walter, the nation that can produce a man such as Saratovsky deserves and some day will win political freedom. I have heard of this Dr. Kharkoff before, too. His life would be a short one if he were in Russia. A remarkable man, who fled after those unfortunate uprisings in 1905. Ah, we are on Fifth Avenue. I suspect that he is taking us to a club on the lower part of the avenue, where a number of the Russian reformers live, patiently waiting and planning for the great 'awakening' in their native land."

Kharkoff's cab had stopped. Our quest had indeed brought us almost to Washington Square. Here we entered an old house of the past generation. As we passed through the wide hall, I noted the high ceilings, the old-fashioned marble mantels stained by time, the long, narrow rooms and dirty-white woodwork, and the threadbare furniture of black walnut and horsehair.

Upstairs in a small back room we found the venerable Saratovsky, tossing, half-delirious with the fever, on a disordered bed. His was a striking figure in this sordid setting, with a high intellectual forehead and deep-set, glowing coals of eyes which gave a hint at the things which had made his life one of the strangest among all the revolutionists of Russia and the works he had done among the most daring. The brown dye was scarcely yet out of his flowing white beard - a relic of his last trip back to his fatherland, where he had eluded the secret police in the disguise of a German gymnasium professor.

Saratovsky extended a thin, hot, emaciated hand to us, and we remained standing. Kennedy said nothing for the moment. The sick man motioned feebly to us to come closer.

"Professor Kennedy," he whispered, "there is some deviltry afoot. The Russian autocracy would stop at nothing. Kharkoff has probably told you of it. I am so weak - "

He groaned and sank back, overcome by a chill that seemed to rack his poor gaunt form.

"Kazanovitch can tell Professor Kennedy something, Doctor. I am too weak to talk, even at this critical time. Take him to see Boris and Ekaterina."

Almost reverently we withdrew, and Kharkoff led us down the hall to another room. The door was ajar, and a light disclosed a man in a Russian peasant's blouse, bending laboriously over a writing-desk. So absorbed was he that not until Kharkoff spoke did he look up. His figure was somewhat slight and his face pointed and of an ascetic mould.

"Ah!" he exclaimed. "You have recalled me from a dream. I fancied I was on the old mir with Ivan, one of my characters. Welcome, comrades."

It flashed over me at once that this was the famous Russian novelist, Boris Kazanovitch. I had not at first connected the name with that of the author of those gloomy tales of peasant life. Kazanovitch stood with his hands tucked under his blouse.

"Night is my favourite time for writing," he explained. "It is then that the imagination works at its best."

I gazed curiously about the room. There seemed to be a marked touch of a woman's hand here and there; it was unmistakable. At last my eye rested on a careless heap of dainty wearing apparel on a chair in the corner.

"Where is Nevsky?" asked Dr. Kharkoff, apparently missing the person who owned the garments.

"Ekaterina has gone to a rehearsal of the little play of Gershuni's escape from Siberia and betrayal by Rosenberg. She will stay with friends on East Broadway to-night. She has deserted me, and here I am all alone, finishing a story for one of the American magazines."

"Ah, Professor Kennedy, that is unfortunate," commented Kharkoff. "A brilliant woman is Mademoiselle Nevsky - devoted to the cause. I know only one who equals her, and that is my patient downstairs, the little dancer, Samarova."

"Samarova is faithful - Nevsky is a genius," put in Kazanovitch. Kharkoff said nothing for a time, though it was easy to see he regarded the actress highly.

"Samarova," he said at length to us, "was arrested for her part in the assassination of Grand Duke Sergius and thrown into solitary confinement in the fortress of St. Peter and St. Paul. They tortured her, the beasts - burned her body with their cigarettes. It was unspeakable. But she would not confess, and finally they had to let her go. Nevsky, who was a student of biology at the University of St. Petersburg when Von Plehve was assassinated, was arrested, but her relatives had sufficient influence to secure her release. They met in Paris, and Nevsky persuaded Olga to go on the stage and come to New York."

"Next to Ekaterina's devotion to the cause is her devotion to science," said Kazanovitch, opening a door to a little room. Then he added: "If she were not a woman, or if your universities were less prejudiced, she would be welcome anywhere as a professor. See, here is her laboratory. It is the best we - she can afford. Organic chemistry, as you call it in English, interests me too, but of course I am not a trained scientist - I am a novelist."

The laboratory was simple, almost bare. Photographs of Koch, Ehrlich, Metchnikoff, and a number of other scientists adorned the walls. The deeply stained deal table was littered with beakers and test-tubes.

"How is Saratovsky?" asked the writer of the doctor, aside, as we gazed curiously about.

Kharkoff shook his head gravely. "We have just come from his room. He was too weak to talk, but he asked that you tell Mr. Kennedy anything that it is necessary he should know about our suspicions."

"It is that we are living with the sword of Damocles constantly dangling over our heads, gentlemen," cried Kazanovitch passionately, turning toward us. "You will excuse me if I get some cigarettes downstairs? Over them I will tell you what we fear."

A call from Saratovsky took the doctor away also at the same moment, and we were left alone.

"A queer situation, Craig," I remarked, glancing involuntarily at the heap of feminine finery on the chair, as I sat down before Kazanovitch's desk.

"Queer for New York; not for St. Petersburg, was his laconic reply, as he looked around for another chair. Everything was littered with books and papers, and at last he leaned over and lifted the dress from the chair to place it on the bed, as the easiest way of securing a seat in the scantily furnished room.

A pocketbook and a letter fell to the floor from the folds of the dress. He stooped to pick them up, and I saw a strange look of surprise on his face. Without a moment's hesitation he shoved the letter into his pocket and replaced the other things as he had found them.

A moment later Kazanovitch returned with a large box of Russian cigarettes. "Be seated, sir," he said to Kennedy, sweeping a mass of books and papers off a large divan. "When Nevsky is not here the room gets sadly disarranged. I have no genius for order."

Amid the clouds of fragrant light smoke we waited for Kazanovitch to break the silence.

"Perhaps you think that the iron hand of the Russian prime minister has broken the backbone of revolution in Russia," he began at length. "But because the Duma is subservient, it does not mean that all is over. Not at all. We are not asleep. Revolution is smouldering, ready to break forth at any moment. The agents of the government know it. They are desperate. There is no means they would not use to crush us. Their long arm reaches even to New York, in this land of freedom."

He rose and excitedly paced the room. Somehow or other, this man did not prepossess me. Was it that I was prejudiced by a puritanical disapproval of the things that pass current in Old World morality? Or was it merely that I found the great writer of fiction seeking the dramatic effect always at the cost of sincerity?

"Just what is it that you suspect?" asked Craig, anxious to dispense with the rhetoric and to get down to facts. "

Surely, when three persons are stricken, you must suspect something."

"Poison," replied Kazanovitch quickly. "Poison, and of a kind that even the poison doctors of St. Petersburg have never employed. Dr. Kharkoff is completely baffled. Your American doctors - two were called in to see Saratovsky - say it is the typhus fever. But Kharkoff knows better. There is no typhus rash. Besides" - and he leaned forward to emphasise his words - " one does not get over typhus in a week and have it again as Saratovsky has." I could see that Kennedy was growing impatient. An idea had occurred to him, and only politeness kept him listening to Kazanovitch longer.

"Doctor," he said, as Kharkoff entered the room again, "do you suppose you could get some perfectly clean test-tubes and sterile bouillon from Miss Nevsky's laboratory? I think I saw a rack of tubes on the table."

"Surely," answered Kharkoff.

"You will excuse us, Mr. Kazanovitch," apologised Kennedy briskly, "but I feel that I am going to have a hard day to-morrow and - by the way, would you be so kind as to come up to my laboratory some time during the day, and continue your story."

On the way out Craig took the doctor aside for a moment, and they talked earnestly. At last Craig motioned to me.

"Walter," he explained, "Dr. Kharkoff is going to prepare some cultures in the test-tubes to-night so that I can make a microscopic examination of the blood of Saratovsky, Samarova, and later of his servant. The tubes will be ready early in the morning, and I have arranged with the doctor for you to call and get them if you have no objection."

I assented, and we started downstairs. As we passed a door on the second floor, a woman's voice called out, "Is that you, Boris?"

"No, Olga, this is Nicholas," replied the doctor. "It is Samarova," he said to us as he entered.

In a few moments he rejoined us. "She is no better," he continued, as we again started away. "I may as well tell you, Professor Kennedy, just how matters stand here. Samarova is head over heels in love with Kazanovitch - you heard her call for him just now? Before they left Paris, Kazanovitch showed some partiality for Olga, but now Nevsky has captured him. She is indeed a fascinating woman, but as for me, if Olga would consent to become Madame Kharkoff, it should be done to-morrow, and she need worry no longer over her broken contract with the American theatre managers. But women are not that way. She prefers the hopeless love. Ah, well, I shall let you know if anything new happens. Good-night, and a thousand thanks for your help, gentlemen."

Nothing was said by either of us on our journey uptown, for it was late and I, at least, was tired.

But Kennedy had no intention of going to bed, I found. Instead, he sat down in his easy chair and shaded his eyes, apparently in deep thought. As I stood by the table to fill my pipe for a last smoke, I saw that he was carefully regarding the letter he had picked up, turning it over and over, and apparently debating with himself what to do with it.

"Some kinds of paper can be steamed open without leaving any trace," he remarked in answer to my unspoken question, laying the letter down before me.

I read the address: "M. Alexander Alexandrovitch Orloff, - Rue de - , Paris, France."

"Letter-opening has been raised to a fine art by the secret service agents of foreign countries," he continued. "Why not take a chance? The simple operation of steaming a letter open is followed by reburnishing the flap with a bone instrument, and no trace is left. I can't do that, for this letter is sealed with wax. One way would be to take a matrix of the seal before breaking the wax and then replace a duplicate of it. No, I won't risk it. I'll try a scientific way."

Between two pieces of smooth wood, Craig laid the letter flat, so that the edges projected about a thirty-second of an inch. He flattened the projecting edge of the envelope, then roughened it, and finally slit it open.

"You see, Walter, later I will place the letter back, apply a hair line of strong white gum, and unite the edges of the envelope under pressure. Let us see what we have here."

He drew out what seemed to be a manuscript on very thin paper, and spread it out flat on the table before us. Apparently it was a scientific paper on a rather unusual subject, "Spontaneous Generation of Life." It was in longhand and read:

*Many thanks for the copy of the paper by Prof. Betallion of Dijon on the artificial fertilization of the eggs of frogs. I consider it a most important advance in the artificial generation of life.

In the printed book this is shown as handwritten

I will not attempt to reproduce in facsimile the entire manuscript, for it is unnecessary, and, in fact, I merely set down part of its contents here because it seemed so utterly valueless to me at the time. It went on to say:

While Betallion punctured the eggs with a platinum needle and developed them by means of electric discharges, Loeb in America placed eggs of the sea-urchin in a strong solution of sea water, then in a bath where they were subjected to the action of butyric acid. Finally they were placed in ordinary sea water again, where they developed in the natural manner. Delage at Roscorf used a liquid containing salts of magnesia and tannate of ammonia to produce the same result.

In his latest book on the Origin of Life Dr. Charlton Bastian tells of using two solutions. One consisted of two or three drops of dilute sodium silicate with eight drops of liquor fern pernitratis to one ounce of distilled water. The other was composed of the same amount of the silicate with six drops of dilute phosphoric acid and six grains of ammonium phosphate. He filled sterilised tubes, sealed them hermetically, and heated them to 125 or 145 degrees, Centigrade, although 60 or 70 degrees would have killed any bacteria remaining in them.

Next he exposed them to sunlight in a south window for from two to four months. When the tubes were opened Dr. Bastian found organisms in them which differed in no way from real bacteria. They grew and multiplied. He contends that he has proved the possibility of spontaneous generation of life.

Then there were the experiments of John Butler Burke of Cambridge, who claimed that he had developed "radiobes" in tubes of sterilised bouillon by means of radium emanations. Daniel Berthelot in France last year announced that he had used the ultra-violet rays to duplicate nature's own process of chlorophyll assimilation. He has broken up carbon dioxide and water-vapour in the air in precisely the same way that the green cells of plants do it.

Leduc at Nantes has made crystals grow from an artificial egg composed of certain chemicals. These crystals show all the apparent vital phenomena without being actually alive. His work is interesting, for it shows the physical forces that probably control minute life cells, once they are created.

"What do you make of it?" asked Kennedy, noting the puzzled look on my face as I finished reading.

"Well, recent research in the problem of the origin of life may be very interesting," I replied. "There are a good many chemicals mentioned here - I wonder if any of them is poisonous? But I am of the opinion that there is something more to this manuscript than a mere scientific paper."

"Exactly, Walter," said Kennedy in half raillery. "What I wanted to know was how you would suggest getting at that something."

Study as I might, I could make nothing out of it. Meanwhile Craig was busily figuring with a piece of paper and a pencil.

"I give it up, Craig," I said at last. "It is late. Perhaps we had better both turn in, and we may have some ideas on it in the morning."

For answer he merely shook his head and continued to scribble and figure on the paper. With a reluctant good-night I shut my door, determined to be up early in the morning and go for the tubes that Kharkoff was to prepare.

But in the morning Kennedy was gone. I dressed hastily, and was just about to go out when he hurried in, showing plainly the effects of having spent a sleepless night. He flung an early edition of a newspaper on the table.

"Too late," he exclaimed. "I tried to reach Kharkoff, but it was too late."

"Another East Side Bomb Outrage," I read. "While returning at a late hour last night from a patient, Dr. Nicholas Kharkoff, of - East Broadway, was severely injured by a bomb which had been placed in his hallway earlier in the evening. Dr. Kharkoff, who is a well-known physician on the East Side, states that he has been constantly shadowed by some one unknown for the past week or two. He attributes his escape with his life to the fact that since he was shadowed he has observed extreme caution. Yesterday his cook was poisoned and is now dangerously ill. Dr. Kharkoff stands high in the Russian community, and it is thought by the police that the bomb was placed by a Russian political agent, as Kharkoff has been active in the ranks of the revolutionists."

"But what made you anticipate it?" I asked of Kennedy, considerably mystified.

"The manuscript," he replied.

"The manuscript? How? Where is it?"

"After I found that it was too late to save Kharkoff and that he was well cared for at the hospital, I hurried to Saratovsky's. Kharkoff had fortunately left the tubes there, and I got them. Here they are. As for the manuscript in the letter, I was going to ask you to slip upstairs by some strategy and return it where I found it, when you went for the tubes this morning. Kazanovitch was out, and I have returned it myself, so you need not go, now."

"He's coming to see you to-day, isn't he?"

"I hope so. I left a note asking him to bring Miss Nevsky, if possible, too. Come, let us breakfast and go over to the laboratory. They may arrive at any moment. Besides, I'm interested to see what the tubes disclose."

Instead of Kazanovitch awaiting us at the laboratory, however, we found Miss Nevsky, haggard and worn. She was a tall, striking girl with more of the Gaul than the Slav in her appearance. There was a slightly sensuous curve to her mouth, but on the whole her face was striking and intellectual. I felt that if she chose she could fascinate a man so that he would dare anything. I never before understood why the Russian police feared the women revolutionists so much. It was because they were themselves, plus every man they could influence.

Nevsky appeared very excited. She talked rapidly, and fire flashed from her grey eyes. "They tell me at the club," she began, " that you are investigating the terrible things that are happening to us. Oh, Professor Kennedy, it is awful! Last night I was staying with some friends on East Broadway. Suddenly we heard a terrific explosion up the street. It was in front of Dr. Kharkoff's house. Thank Heaven, he is still alive! But I was so unnerved I could not sleep. I fancied I might be the next to go.

"Early this morning I hastened to return to Fifth Avenue. As I entered the door of my room I could not help thinking of the horrible fate of Dr. Kharkoff. For some unknown reason, just as I was about to push the door farther open, I hesitated and looked - I almost fainted. There stood another bomb just inside. If I had moved the door a fraction of an inch it would have exploded. I screamed, and Olga, sick as she was, ran to my assistance - or perhaps she thought something had happened to Boris. It is standing there yet. None of us dares touch it. Oh, Professor Kennedy, it is dreadful, dreadful. And I cannot find Boris - Mr. Kazanovitch, I mean. Saratovsky, who is like a father to us all, is scarcely able to speak. Dr. Kharkoff is helpless in the hospital. Oh, what are we to do, what are we to do?"

She stood trembling before us, imploring.

"Calm yourself, Miss Nevsky," said Kennedy in a reassuring tone. "Sit down and let us plan. I take it that it was a chemical bomb and not one with a fuse, or you would have a different story to tell. First of all, we must remove it. That is easily done."

He called up a near-by garage and ordered an automobile. "I will drive it myself," he ordered, "only send a man around with it immediately."

"No, no, no," she cried, running toward him, you must not risk it. It is bad enough that we should risk our lives. But strangers must not. Think, Professor Kennedy. Suppose the bomb should explode at a touch! Had we not better call the police and let them take the risk, even if it does get into the papers?"

"No," replied Kennedy firmly. "Miss Nevsky, I am quite willing to take the risk. Besides, here comes the automobile."

"You are too kind," she exclaimed. "Kazanovitch himself could do no more. How am I ever to thank you?"

On the back of the automobile Kennedy placed a peculiar oblong box, swung on two concentric rings balanced on pivots, like a most delicate compass.

We rode quickly downtown, and Kennedy hurried into the house, bidding us stand back. With a long pair of tongs he seized the bomb firmly. It was a tense moment. Suppose his hand should unnecessarily tremble, or he should tip it just a bit - it might explode and blow him to atoms. Keeping it perfectly horizontal he carried it carefully out to the waiting automobile and placed it gingerly in the box.

"Wouldn't it be a good thing to fill the box with water?" I suggested, having read somewhere that that was the usual way of opening a bomb, under water.

"No," he replied, as he closed the lid, "that wouldn't do any good with a bomb of this sort. It would explode under water just as well as in air. This is a safety bomb-carrier. It is known as the Cardon suspension. It was invented by Professor Cardono, an Italian. You see, it is always held in a perfectly horizontal position, no matter how you jar it. I am now going to take the bomb to some safe and convenient place where I can examine it at my leisure. Meanwhile, Miss Nevsky, I will leave you in charge of Mr. Jameson."

"Thank you so much," she said. "I feel better now. I didn't dare go into my own room with that bomb at the door. If Mr. Jameson can only find out what has become of Mr. Kazanovitch, that is all I want. What do you suppose has happened to him? Is he, too, hurt or ill?"

"Very well, then," Craig replied. " I will commission you, Walter, to find Kazanovitch. I shall be back again shortly before noon to examine the wreck of Kharkoff's office. Meet me there. Goodbye, Miss Nevsky."

It was not the first time that I had had a roving commission to find some one who had disappeared in New

York. I started by inquiring for every possible place that he might be found. No one at the Fifth Avenue house could tell me anything definite, though they were able to give me a number of places where he was known. I consumed practically the whole morning going from one place to another on the East Side. Some of the picturesque haunts of the revolutionists would have furnished material for a story in themselves. But nowhere had they any word of Kazanovitch, until I visited a Polish artist who was illustrating his stories. He had been there, looking very worn and tired, and had talked vacantly about the sketches which the artist had showed him. After that I lost all trace of him again. It was nearly noon as I hurried to meet Craig at Kharkoff's.

Imagine my surprise to see Kazanovitch already there, seated in the wrecked office, furiously smoking cigarettes and showing evident signs of having something very disturbing on his mind. The moment he caught sight of me, he hurried forward.

"Is Professor Kennedy coming soon?" he inquired eagerly. "I was going up to his laboratory, but I called up Nevsky, and she said he would be here at noon." Then he put his hand up to my ear and whispered, "I have found out who it was who shadowed Kharkoff."

"Who?" I asked, saying nothing of my long search of the morning.

23

"His name is Revalenko - Feodor Revalenko. I saw him standing across the street in front of the house last night after you had gone. When Kharkoff left, he followed him. I hurried out quietly and followed both of them. Then the explosion came. This man slipped down a narrow street as soon as he saw Kharkoff fall. As people were running to Kharkoff's assistance, I did the same. He saw me following him and ran, and I ran, too, and overtook him. Mr. Jameson, when I looked into his face I could not believe it. Revalenko - he is one of the most ardent members of our organisation. He would not tell me why he had followed Kharkoff. I could make him confess nothing. But I am sure he is an agent provocateur of the Russian government, that he is secretly giving away the plans that we are making, everything. We have a plot on now - perhaps he has informed them of that. Of course he denied setting the bomb or trying to poison any of us, but he was very frightened. I shall denounce him at the first opportunity."

I said nothing. Kazanovitch regarded me keenly to see what impression the story made on me, but I did not let my looks betray anything, except proper surprise, and he seemed satisfied.

It might be true, after all, I reasoned, the more I thought of it. I had heard that the Russian consul-general had a very extensive spy system in the city. In fact, even that morning I had had pointed out to me some spies at work in the public libraries, watching what young Russians were reading. I did not doubt that there were spies in the very inner circle of the revolutionists themselves.

At last Kennedy appeared. While Kazanovitch poured forth his story, with here and there, I fancied, an elaboration of a particularly dramatic point, Kennedy quickly examined the walls and floor of the wrecked office with his magnifying-glass. When he had concluded his search, he turned to Kazanovitch.

"Would it be possible," he asked, "to let this Revalenko believe that he could trust you, that it would be safe for him to visit you to-night at Saratovsky's? Surely you can find some way of reassuring him."

"Yes, I think that can be arranged," said Kazanovitch. "I will go to him, will make him think I have misunderstood him, that I have not lost faith in him, provided he can explain all. He will come. Trust me."

"Very well, then. To-night at eight I shall be there," promised Kennedy, as the novelist and he shook hands.

"What do you think of the Revalenko story?" I asked of Craig, as we started uptown again.

"Anything is possible in this case," he answered sententiously.

"Well," I exclaimed, "this all is truly Russian. For intrigue they are certainly the leaders of the world to-day. There is only one person that I have any real confidence in, and that is old Saratovsky himself. Somebody is playing traitor, Craig. Who is it?"

"That is what science will tell us to-night," was his brief reply. There was no getting anything out of Craig until he was absolutely sure that his proofs had piled up irresistibly.

Promptly at eight we met at the old house on Fifth Avenue. Kharkoff's wounds had proved less severe than had at first been suspected, and, having recovered from the shock, he insisted on being transferred from the hospital in a private ambulance so that he could be near his friends. Saratovsky, in spite of his high fever, ordered that the door to his room be left open and his bed moved so that he could hear and see what passed in the room down the hall. Nevsky was there and Kazanovitch, and even brave Olga Samarova, her pretty face burning with the fever, would not be content until she was carried upstairs, although Dr. Kharkoff protested vigorously that it might have fatal consequences. Revalenko, an enigma of a man, sat stolidly. The only thing I noticed about him was an occasional look of malignity at Nevsky and Kazanovitch when he thought he was unobserved.

It was indeed a strange gathering, the like of which the old house had never before harboured in all its varied history. Every one was on the qui vive, as Kennedy placed on the table a small wire basket containing some test-tubes, each tube corked with a small wadding of cotton. There was also a receptacle holding a dozen glass-handled platinum wires, a microscope, and a number of slides. The bomb, now rendered innocuous by having been crushed in a huge hydraulic press, lay in fragments in the box.

"First, I want you to consider the evidence of the bomb," began Kennedy. "No crime, I firmly believe, is ever perpetrated without leaving some clue. The slightest trace, even a drop of blood no larger than a pin-head, may suffice to convict a murderer. The impression made on a cartridge by the hammer of a pistol, or a single hair found on the clothing of a suspected person, may serve as valid proof of crime.

"Until lately, however, science was powerless against the bomb-thrower. A bomb explodes into a thousand parts, and its contents suddenly become gaseous. You can't collect and investigate the gases. Still, the bomb-thrower is sadly deceived if he believes the bomb leaves no trace for the scientific detective. It is difficult for the chemist to find out the secrets of a shattered bomb. But it can be done.

"I examined the walls of Dr. Kharkoff's house, and fortunately was able to pick out a few small fragments of the contents of the bomb which had been thrown out before the flame ignited them. I have analysed them, and find them to be a peculiar species of blasting-gelatine. It is made at only one factory in this country, and I have a list of purchasers for some time back. One name, or rather the description of an assumed name, in the list agrees with other evidence I have been able to collect. Moreover, the explosive was placed in a lead tube. Lead tubes are common enough. However, there is no need of further evidence."

He paused, and the revolutionists stared fixedly at the fragments of the now harmless bomb before them.

"The exploded bomb," concluded Craig, "was composed of the same materials as this, which I found unexploded at the door of Miss Nevsky's room - the same sort of lead tube, the same blasting-gelatine. The fuse, a long cord saturated in sulphur, was merely a blind. The real method of explosion was by means of a chemical contained in a glass tube which was inserted after the bomb was put in place. The least jar, such as opening a door, which would tip the bomb ever so little out of the horizontal, was all that was necessary to explode it. The exploded bomb and the unexploded were in all respects identical - the same hand set both."

A gasp of astonishment ran through the circle. Could it be that one of their own number was playing false? In at least this instance in the warfare of the chemist and the dynamiter the chemist had come out ahead.

"But," Kennedy hurried along, "the thing that interests me most about this case is not the evidence of the bombs. Bombs are common enough weapons, after all. It is the evidence of almost diabolical cunning that has been shown in the effort to get rid of the father of the revolution, as you like to call him."

Craig cleared his throat and played with our feelings as a cat does with a mouse. "Strange to say, the most deadly, the most insidious, the most elusive agency for committing murder is one that can be obtained and distributed with practically no legal restrictions. Any doctor can purchase disease germs in quantities sufficient to cause thousands and thousands of deaths without giving any adequate explanation for what purpose he requires them. More than that, any person claiming to be a scientist or having some acquaintance with science and scientists can usually obtain germs without difficulty. Every pathological laboratory contains stores of disease germs, neatly sealed up in test-tubes, sufficient to depopulate whole cities and even nations. With almost no effort, I myself have actually cultivated enough germs to kill every person within a radius of a mile of the Washington Arch down the street. They are here in these test-tubes."

We scarcely breathed. Suppose Kennedy should let loose this deadly foe, these germs of death, whatever they were? Yet that was precisely what some fiend incarnate had done, and that fiend was sitting in the room with us.

"Here I have one of the most modern dark-field microscopes," he resumed. "On this slide I have placed a little pin-point of a culture made from the blood of Saratovsky. I will stain the culture. Now - er - Walter, look through the microscope under this powerful light and tell us what you see on the slide."

I bent over. "In the darkened field I see a number of germs like dancing points of coloured light," I said. "They are wriggling about with a peculiar twisting motion."

"Like a corkscrew," interrupted Kennedy, impatient to go on. "They are of the species known as Spirilla. Here is another slide, a culture from the blood of Samarova."

"I see them there, too," I exclaimed.

Every one was now crowding about for a glimpse, as I raised my head.

"What is this germ?" asked a hollow voice from the doorway.

We looked, startled. There stood Saratovsky, more like a ghost than a living being. Kennedy sprang forward and caught him as he swayed, and I moved up an armchair for him.

It is the spirillum Obermeieri," said Kennedy, "the germ of the relapsing fever, but of the most virulent Asiatic strain. Obermeyer, who discovered it, caught the disease and died of it, a martyr to science."

A shriek of consternation rang forth from Samarova. The rest of us paled, but repressed our feelings.

One moment," added Kennedy hastily. "Don't be unnecessarily alarmed. I have something more to say. Be calm for a moment longer."

He unrolled a blue-print and placed it on the table.

"This," he continued, "is the photographic copy of a message which, I suppose, is now on its way to the Russian minister to France in Paris. Some one in this room besides Mr. Jameson and myself has seen this letter before. I will hold it up as I pass around and let each one see it.

In intense silence Kennedy passed before each of us, holding up the blue-print and searchingly scanning the faces. No one betrayed by any sign that he recognised it. At last it came to Revalenko himself.

"The checkerboard, the checkerboard!" he cried, his eyes half starting from their sockets as he gazed at it.

"Yes," said Kennedy in a low tone, "the checkerboard. It took me some time to figure it out. It is a cipher that would have baffled Poe. In fact, there is no means of deciphering it unless you chance to know its secret. I happened to have heard of it a long time ago abroad, yet my recollection was vague, and I had to reconstruct it with much difficulty. It took me all night to do it. It is a cipher, however, that is well known among the official classes of Russia.

"Fortunately I remember the crucial point, without which I should still be puzzling over it. It is that a perfectly innocent message, on its face, may be used to carry a secret, hidden message. The letters which compose the words, instead of being written continuously along, as we ordinarily write, have, as you will observe if you look twice, breaks, here and there. These breaks in the letters stand for numbers.

"Thus the first words are 'Many thanks.' The first break is at the end of the letter 'n,' between it and the 'y.' There are three letters before this break. That stands for the number 3.

"When you come to the end of a word, if the stroke is down at the end of the last letter, that means no break; if it is up, it means a break. The stroke at the end of the 'y' is plainly down. Therefore there is no break until after the 't.' That gives us the number 2. So we get 1 next, and again 1, and still again 1; then 5; then 5; then 1; and so on.

"Now, take these numbers in pairs, thus 3 - 2; 1 - 1; 1 - 5; 5 - 1. By consulting this table you can arrive at the hidden message.

He held up a cardboard bearing the following arrangement of the letters of the alphabet:

	1	2	3	4	5
1	A	B	C	D	E
2	F	G	H	IJ	K
3	L	M	N	O	P
4	Q	R	S	T	U
5	V	W	X	Y	Z

"Thus," he continued, "3 - 2 means the third column and second line. That is 'H.' Then 1 - 1 is 'A'; 1 - 5 is 'V'; 5 - 1 is 'E' - and we get the word 'Have.'"

Not a soul stirred as Kennedy unfolded the cipher. What was the terrible secret in that scientific essay I had puzzled so unsuccessfully over, the night before?

"Even this can be complicated by choosing a series of fixed numbers to be added to the real numbers over and over again, Or the order of the alphabet can be changed. However, we have the straight cipher only to deal with here."

"And what for Heaven's sake does it reveal?" asked Saratovsky, leaning forward, forgetful of the fever that was consuming him.

Kennedy pulled out a piece of paper on which he had written the hidden message and read:

"Have successfully inoculated S. with fever. Public opinion America would condemn violence. Think best death should appear natural. Samarova infected also. Cook unfortunately took dose in food intended Kharkoff. Now have three cases. Shall stop there at present. Dangerous excite further suspicion health authorities."

Rapidly I eliminated in my mind the persons mentioned, as Craig read. Saratovsky of course was not guilty, for the plot had centred about him. Nor was little Samarova, nor Dr. Kharkoff. I noted Revalenko and Kazanovitch glaring at each other and hastily tried to decide which I more strongly suspected.

"Will get K.," continued Kennedy. "Think bomb perhaps all right. K. case different from S. No public sentiment."

"So Kharkoff had been marked for slaughter," I thought. Or was "K." Kazanovitch? I regarded Revalenko more closely. He was suspiciously sullen.

"Must have more money. Cable ten thousand rubles at once Russian consul-general. Will advise you plot against Czar as details perfected here. Expect break up New York band with death of S."

If Kennedy himself had thrown a bomb or scattered broadcast the contents of the test-tubes, the effect could not have been more startling than his last quiet sentence - and sentence it was in two senses.

"Signed," he said, folding the paper up deliberately, "Ekaterina Nevsky."

It was as if a cable had snapped and a weight had fallen. Revalenko sprang up and grasped Kazanovitch by the hand. "Forgive me, comrade, for ever suspecting you," he cried.

"And forgive me for suspecting you," replied Kazanovitch, "but how did you come to shadow Kharkoff?"

"I ordered him to follow Kharkoff secretly and protect him," explained Saratovsky.

Olga and Ekaterina faced each other fiercely. Olga was trembling with emotion. Nevsky stood coldly, defiantly. If ever there was a consummate actress it was she, who had put the bomb at her own door and had rushed off to start Kennedy on a blind trail.

"You traitress," cried Olga passionately, forgetting all in her outraged love. "You won his affections from me by your false beauty - yet all the time you would have killed him like a dog for the Czar's gold. At last you are unmasked - you Azeff in skirts. False friend - you would have killed us all - Saratovsky, Kharkoff

"Be still, little fool," exclaimed Nevsky contemptuously. "The spirilla fever has affected your brains. Bah! I will not stay with those who are so ready to suspect an old comrade on the mere word of a charlatan. Boris Kazanovitch, do you stand there silent and let this insult be heaped upon me?"

For answer, Kazanovitch deliberately turned his back on his lover of a moment ago and crossed the room. "Olga," he pleaded, "I have been a fool. Some day I may be worthy of your love. Fever or not, I must beg your forgiveness."

With a cry of delight the actress flung her arms about Boris, as he imprinted a penitent kiss on her warm lips.

"Simpleton," hissed Nevsky with curling lips. "Now you, too, will die."

"One moment, Ekaterina Nevsky," interposed Kennedy, as he picked up some vacuum tubes full of a golden-yellow powder, that lay on the table. "The spirilla, as scientists now know, belong to the same family as those which cause what we call, euphemistically, the 'black plague.' It is the same species as that of the African sleeping sickness and the Philippine yaws. Last year a famous doctor whose photograph I see in the next room, Dr. Ehrlich of Frankfort, discovered a cure for all these diseases. It will rid the blood of your victims of the Asiatic relapsing fever germs in forty-eight hours. In these tubes I have the now famous salvarsan."

With a piercing shriek of rage at seeing her deadly work so quickly and completely undone, Nevsky flung herself into the little laboratory behind her and bolted the door.

Her face still wore the same cold, contemptuous smile, as Kennedy gently withdrew a sharp scalpel from her breast.

"Perhaps it is best this way, after all," he said simply.